Kitty's New Doll

By Dorothy M. Kunhardt

Illustrated by Lucinda McQueen

78244

A GOLDEN BOOK, NEW YORK

Western Publishing Company, Inc.

Racine, Wisconsin 53404

Kitty and her mother were going to the toy store.
"You may choose your very own doll," said Mother. "Choose
the one you like best."

At the toy store there were long rows of beautiful dolls.

There was a doll that
could wiggle his whiskers
and switch his tail.

There was a doll that
could close her eyes and say,
"Ma-ma."

There was a soldier doll
and a Boy Scout doll and
a nurse doll.

There was a grandmother
doll with glasses and
a grandfather doll with
a pocket watch.

There was a doll that
could really walk and a doll
you could give a bath to.

There was a baby doll
that could drink water from
a bottle and wet her diaper.

There was an orange doll and a gray doll and a white doll.
There was a doll with black fur and white spots.
All the dolls were so wonderful it was hard for Kitty to
choose.

Then, at the end of the row, Kitty saw a rag doll.
The rag doll was made of cloth stuffed with cotton. Her
face was painted on. Her fur was painted on. Her clothes were
painted on. She couldn't do a single thing, not even sleep.

Kitty thought the rag doll looked as if she were saying,
"Choose me. Oh, please choose me."
Kitty picked up the rag doll and held her in her arms.

"Mother, please, I want this doll," said Kitty.
"Are you sure?" asked Mother. "Wouldn't you rather have a doll that can close her eyes and go to sleep? Or a pretty doll with a long tail just like yours? Do you really want a plain old rag doll that can't do anything at all?"

"She isn't plain," said Kitty. "She can switch her pretend tail and wiggle her pretend whiskers...

...and drink from her pretend bottle.

She can pretend cry
and pretend sleep."

"And do you know what
I like best of all?"
"What?" asked Mother.
"She can say anything I want
her to say," said Kitty.

"All right," said Mother. "We'll buy her, and she'll be your very own."

Mother paid for the rag doll.

"Now you're her mother," she said to Kitty.

The two mothers walked home. Kitty hugged
her rag doll. She was pretending the rag doll said,
"I love you, Mother."